S0-CFI-094

There now arose a mighty storm, and he was tossed this way and that.
[See page 70.]

Peter Pan in Kensington Gardens

By

J. M. Barrie

Illustrated by

Arthur Rackham

Dover Publications, Inc.
Mineola, New York

TO SYLVIA AND ARTHUR LLEWELYN DAVIES AND THEIR BOYS (MY BOYS)

Copyright

Bibliographical Note

This Dover edition, first published in 2008, is an unabridged republication of the work originally published by Charles Scribner's Sons, New York, in 1907. The fifty color plates from the original edition have been interspersed throughout the text for the Dover edition.

Library of Congress Cataloging-in-Publication Data

Barrie, J. M. (James Matthew), 1860–1937.
Peter Pan in Kensington Gardens / J. M. Barrie ; illustrated by Arthur Rackham.
p. cm.
"This Dover edition, first published in 2008, is an unabridged republication of the work originally published by Charles Scribner's Sons, New York, in 1907. The fifty color plates from the original edition have been interspersed throughout the text for the Dover edition"—T. p. verso.
ISBN-13: 978-0-486-46607-1
ISBN-10: 0-486-46607-8
1. Peter Pan (Fictitious character) — Fiction. 2. Kensington Gardens (London, England — Fiction. I. Title.

PR4074.P318 2008
823'.912—dc22

2008020633

Manufactured in the United States of America
Dover Publications, Inc., 31 East 2nd Street, Mineola, N.Y. 11501

Contents

List of Illustrations

List of Illustrations

List of Illustrations

Peter Pan
in Kensington Gardens

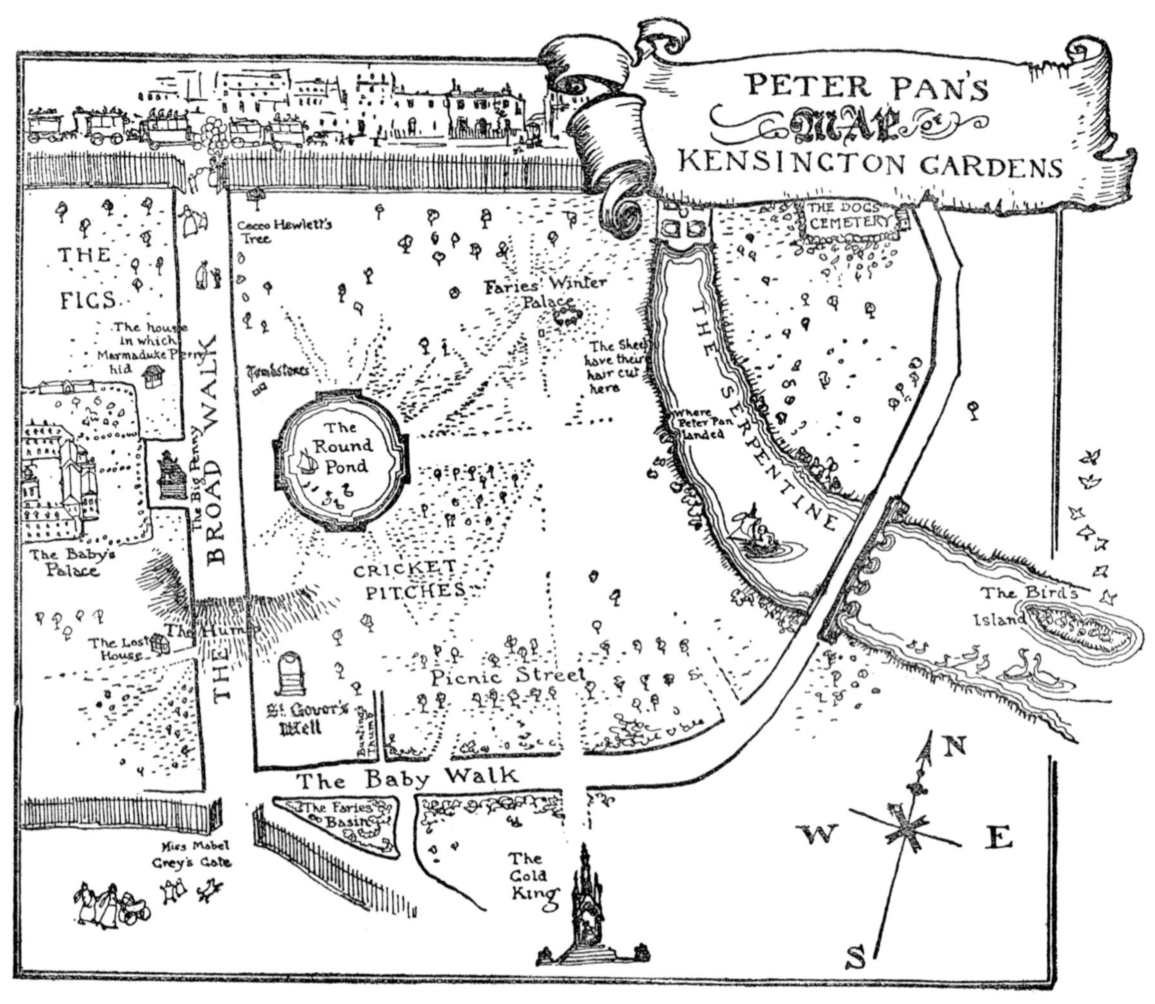

Peter Pan's Map of Kensington Gardens

I
The Grand Tour of the Gardens

YOU must see for yourselves that it will be difficult to follow Peter Pan's adventures unless you are familiar with the Kensington Gardens. They are in London, where the King lives, and I used to take David there nearly every day unless he was looking decidedly flushed. No child has ever been in the whole of the Gardens, because it is so soon time to turn back. The reason it is soon time to turn back is that, if you are as small as David, you sleep from twelve to one. If your mother was not so sure that you sleep from twelve to one, you could most likely see the whole of them.

The Kensington Gardens are in London, where the King lives.
[See page 1.]

The Gardens are bounded on one side by a never-ending line of omnibuses, over which your nurse has such authority that if she holds up her finger to any one of them it stops immediately. She then crosses with you in safety to the other side. There are more gates to the Gardens than one gate, but that is the one you go in at, and before you go in you speak to the lady with the balloons, who sits just outside. This is as near to being inside as she may venture, because, if she were to let go her hold of the railings for one moment, the balloons would lift her up, and she would be flown away. She sits very squat, for the balloons are always tugging at her, and the strain has given her quite a red face. Once she was a new one, because the old one had let go, and David was very sorry for the old one, but as she did let go, he wished he had been there to see.

The Gardens are a tremendous big place, with millions and hundreds of trees; and first

The lady with the balloons, who sits just outside.
[See page 3.]

you come to the Figs, but you scorn to loiter there, for the Figs is the resort of superior little persons, who are forbidden to mix with the commonalty, and is so named, according to legend, because they dress in full fig. These dainty ones are themselves contemptuously called Figs by David and other heroes, and you have a key to the manners and customs of this dandiacal section of the Gardens when I tell you that cricket is called crickets here. Occasionally a rebel Fig climbs over the fence into the world, and such a one was Miss Mabel Grey, of whom I shall tell you when we come to Miss Mabel Grey's gate. She was the only really celebrated Fig.

We are now in the Broad Walk, and it is as much bigger than the other walks as your father is bigger than you. David wondered if it began little, and grew and grew, until it was quite grown up, and whether the other walks are its babies, and he drew a picture, which diverted him very much, of the Broad Walk

In the Broad Walk you meet all the people who are worth knowing.
[See page 7.]

giving a tiny walk an airing in a perambulator. In the Broad Walk you meet all the people who are worth knowing, and there is usually a grown-up with them to prevent them going on the damp grass, and to make them stand disgraced at the corner of a seat if they have been mad-dog or Mary-Annish. To be Mary-Annish is to behave like a girl, whimpering because nurse won't carry you, or simpering with your thumb in your mouth, and it is a hateful quality; but to be mad-dog is to kick out at everything, and there is some satisfaction in that.

If I were to point out all the notable places as we pass up the Broad Walk, it would be time to turn back before we reach them, and I simply wave my stick at Cecco Hewlett's Tree, that memorable spot where a boy called Cecco lost his penny, and, looking for it, found twopence. There has been a good deal of excavation going on there ever since. Farther up the walk is the little wooden house in which

The Hump, which is the part of the Broad Walk where all the big races are run.
[See page 11.]

Marmaduke Perry hid. There is no more awful story of the Gardens than this of Marmaduke Perry, who had been Mary-Annish three days in succession, and was sentenced to appear in the Broad Walk dressed in his sister's clothes. He hid in the little wooden house, and refused to emerge until they brought him knickerbockers with pockets.

You now try to go to the Round Pond, but nurses hate it, because they are not really manly, and they make you look the other way, at the Big Penny and the Baby's Palace. She was the most celebrated baby of the Gardens, and lived in the palace all alone, with ever so many dolls, so people rang the bell, and up she got out of her bed, though it was past six o'clock, and she lighted a candle and opened the door in her nighty, and then they all cried with great rejoicings, "Hail, Queen of England!" What puzzled David most was how she knew where the matches were kept. The Big Penny is a statue about her.

There is almost nothing that has such a keen sense of fun as a fallen leaf.
[See page 11.]

Next we come to the Hump, which is the part of the Broad Walk where all the big races are run; and even though you had no intention of running you do run when you come to the Hump, it is such a fascinating, slide-down kind of place. Often you stop when you have run about half-way down it, and then you are lost; but there is another little wooden house near here, called the Lost House, and so you tell the man that you are lost and then he finds you. It is glorious fun racing down the Hump, but you can't do it on windy days because then you are not there, but the fallen leaves do it instead of you. There is almost nothing that has such a keen sense of fun as a fallen leaf.

From the Hump we can see the gate that is called after Miss Mabel Grey, the Fig I promised to tell you about. There were always two nurses with her, or else one mother and one nurse, and for a long time she was a pattern-child who always coughed off the table and said, "How do you do?" to the other

Figs, and the only game she played at was flinging a ball gracefully and letting the nurse bring it back to her. Then one day she tired of it all and went mad-dog, and, first, to show that she really was mad-dog, she unloosened both her boot-laces and put out her tongue east, west, north, and south. She then flung her sash into a puddle and danced on it till dirty water was squirted over her frock, after which she climbed the fence and had a series of incredible adventures, one of the least of which was that she kicked off both her boots. At last she came to the gate that is now called after her, out of which she ran into streets David and I have never been in though we have heard them roaring, and still she ran on and would never again have been heard of had not her mother jumped into a 'bus and thus overtaken her. It all happened, I should say, long ago, and this is not the Mabel Grey whom David knows.

Returning up the Broad Walk we have on

our right the Baby Walk, which is so full of perambulators that you could cross from side to side stepping on babies, but the nurses won't let you do it. From this walk a passage called Bunting's Thumb, because it is that length, leads into Picnic Street, where there are real kettles, and chestnut-blossom falls into your mug as you are drinking. Quite common children picnic here also, and the blossom falls into their mugs just the same.

Next comes St. Govor's Well, which was full of water when Malcolm the Bold fell into it. He was his mother's favourite, and he let her put her arm round his neck in public because she was a widow; but he was also partial to adventures, and liked to play with a chimney-sweep who had killed a good many bears. The sweep's name was Sooty, and one day, when they were playing near the well, Malcolm fell in and would have been drowned had not Sooty dived in and rescued him; and the water had washed Sooty clean, and he now stood revealed as Malcolm's long-lost father. So Malcolm would not let his mother put her arm round his neck any more.

Between the well and the Round Pond are the cricket pitches, and frequently the choosing of sides exhausts so much time that there is scarcely any cricket. Everybody wants to bat first, and as soon as he is out he bowls unless you are the better wrestler, and while you are wrestling with him the fielders have scattered to play at something else. The Gardens are noted for two kinds of cricket: boy cricket, which is real cricket with a bat, and girl cricket, which is with a racquet and the governess. Girls can't really play cricket, and when you are watching their futile efforts you make funny sounds at them. Nevertheless, there was a very disagreeable incident one day when some forward girls challenged David's team, and a disturbing creature called Angela Clare sent down so many yorkers that— However, instead of telling you the result of that regrettable match I shall pass on hurriedly to the Round Pond, which is the wheel that keeps all the Gardens going.

It is round because it is in the very middle of the Gardens, and when you are come to it you never want to go any farther. You can't be good all the time at the Round Pond, however much you try. You can be good in the Broad Walk all the time, but not at the Round Pond, and the reason is that you forget, and, when you remember, you are so wet that you may as well be wetter. There are men who sail boats on the Round Pond, such big boats that they bring them in barrows, and sometimes in perambulators, and then the baby has to walk. The bow-legged children in the Gardens are those who had to walk too soon because their father needed the perambulator.

You always want to have a yacht to sail on the Round Pond, and in the end your uncle gives you one; and to carry it to the Pond the first day is splendid, also to talk about it to boys who have no uncle is splendid, but soon you like to leave it at home. For the sweetest craft that slips her moorings in the Round Pond is what is called a stick-boat, because she is rather like a stick until she is in the water and you are holding the string. Then as you walk round, pulling her, you see little men running about her deck, and sails rise magically and catch the breeze, and you put in on dirty nights at snug harbours which are unknown to the lordly yachts. Night passes in a twink, and again your rakish craft noses for the wind, whales spout, you glide over buried cities, and have brushes with pirates, and cast anchor on coral isles. You are a solitary boy while all this is taking place, for two boys together cannot adventure far upon the Round Pond, and though you may talk to yourself throughout the voyage, giving orders and executing them with despatch, you know not, when it is time to go home, where you have been or what swelled your sails; your treasure-trove is all locked away in your hold, so to speak, which will be opened, perhaps, by another little boy many years afterwards.

But those yachts have nothing in their hold. Does any one return to this haunt of his youth because of the yachts that used to sail it? Oh no. It is the stick-boat that is freighted with memories. The yachts are toys, their owner a fresh-water mariner; they can cross and recross a pond only while the stick-boat goes to sea. You yachtsmen with your wands, who think we are all there to gaze on you, your ships are only accidents of this place, and were they all to be boarded and sunk by the ducks, the real business of the Round Pond would be carried on as usual.

Paths from everywhere crowd like children to the pond. Some of them are ordinary paths, which have a rail on each side, and are made by men with their coats off, but others are vagrants, wide at one spot and at another so narrow that you can stand astride them.

They are called Paths that have Made Themselves, and David did wish he could see them doing it. But, like all the most wonderful things that happen in the Gardens, it is done, we concluded, at night after the gates are closed. We have also decided that the paths make themselves because it is their only chance of getting to the Round Pond.

One of these gypsy paths comes from the place where the sheep get their hair cut. When David shed his curls at the hairdresser's, I am told, he said good-bye to them without a tremor, though his mother has never been quite the same bright creature since; so he despises the sheep as they run from their shearer, and calls out tauntingly, "Cowardy, cowardy custard!" But when the man grips them between his legs David shakes a fist at him for using such big scissors. Another startling moment is when the man turns back the grimy wool from the sheep's shoulders and they look suddenly like ladies in the stalls of a theatre. The sheep are so frightened by the shearing that it makes them quite white and thin, and as soon as they are set free they begin to nibble the grass at once, quite anxiously, as if they feared that they would never be worth eating. David wonders whether they know each other, now that they are so different, and if it makes them fight with the wrong ones. They are great fighters, and thus so unlike country sheep that every year they give my St. Bernard dog, Porthos, a shock. He can make a field of country sheep fly by merely announcing his approach, but these town sheep come toward him with no promise of gentle entertainment, and then a light from last year breaks upon Porthos. He cannot with dignity retreat, but he stops and looks about him as if lost in admiration of the

The Serpentine begins near here. It is a lovely lake, and there is a drowned forest at the bottom of it. If you peer over the edge you can see the trees all growing upside down, and they say that at night there are also drowned stars in it. [See page 22.]

The fairies of the Serpentine.
[See page 22.]

scenery, and presently he strolls away with a fine indifference and a glint at me from the corner of his eye.

The Serpentine begins near here. It is a lovely lake, and there is a drowned forest at the bottom of it. If you peer over the edge you can see the trees all growing upside down, and they say that at night there are also drowned stars in it. If so, Peter Pan sees them when he is sailing across the lake in the Thrush's Nest. A small part only of the Serpentine is in the Gardens, for soon it passes beneath a bridge to far away where the island is on which all the birds are born that become baby boys and girls. No one who is human, except Peter Pan (and he is only half human), can land on the island, but you may write what you want (boy or girl, dark or fair) on a piece of paper, and then twist it into the shape of a boat and slip it into the water, and it reaches Peter Pan's island after dark.

We are on the way home now, though of

The island on which all the birds are born that become baby boys and girls.
[See page 22.]

course, it is all pretence that we can go to so many of the places in one day. I should have had to be carrying David long ago, and resting on every seat like old Mr. Salford. That was what we called him, because he always talked to us of a lovely place called Salford where he had been born. He was a crab-apple of an old gentleman who wandered all day in the Gardens from seat to seat trying to fall in with somebody who was acquainted with the town of Salford, and when we had known him for a year or more we actually did meet another aged solitary who had once spent Saturday to Monday in Salford. He was meek and timid and carried his address inside his hat, and whatever part of London he was in search of he always went to Westminster Abbey first as a starting-point. Him we carried in triumph to our other friend, with the story of that Saturday to Monday, and never shall I forget the gloating joy with which Mr. Salford leapt at him. They have been cronies ever since,

Old Mr. Salford was a crab-apple of an old gentleman who wandered all day in the Gardens.
[See page 24.]

and I notice that Mr. Salford, who naturally does most of the talking, keeps tight grip of the other old man's coat.

The two last places before you come to our gate are the Dog's Cemetery and the chaffinch's nest, but we pretend not to know what the Dog's Cemetery is, as Porthos is always with us. The nest is very sad. It is quite white, and the way we found it was wonderful. We were having another look among the bushes for David's lost worsted ball, and instead of the ball we found a lovely nest made of the worsted, and containing four eggs, with scratches on them very like David's handwriting, so we think they must have been the mother's love-letters to the little ones inside. Every day we were in the Gardens we paid a call at the nest, taking care that no cruel boy should see us, and we dropped crumbs, and soon the bird knew us as friends, and sat in the nest looking at us kindly with her shoulders hunched up. But one day when we went there were only two eggs in the nest, and the next time there were none. The saddest part of it was that the poor little chaffinch fluttered about the bushes, looking so reproachfully at us that we knew she thought we had done it; and though David tried to explain to her, it was so long since he had spoken the bird language that I fear she did not understand. He and I left the Gardens that day with our knuckles in our eyes.

II
Peter Pan

If you ask your mother whether she knew about Peter Pan when she was a little girl, she will say, "Why, of course, I did, child"; and if you ask her whether he rode on a goat in those days, she will say, "What a foolish question to ask; certainly he did." Then if you ask your grandmother whether she knew about Peter Pan when she was a girl, she also says, "Why, of course I did, child," but if you ask her whether he rode on a goat in those days, she says she never heard of his having a goat. Perhaps she has forgotten, just as she sometimes forgets your name and calls you Mildred, which is your mother's name. Still, she could hardly forget such an important thing as the goat. Therefore there was no goat when your grandmother was a little girl. This shows that, in telling the story of Peter Pan, to begin with the goat (as most people do) is as silly as to put on your jacket before your vest.

Of course, it also shows that Peter is ever so old, but he is really always the same age, so that does not matter in the least. His age is one week, and though he was born so long ago he has never had a birthday, nor is there the slightest chance of his ever having one. The reason is that he escaped from being a human when he was seven days old; he escaped by the window and flew back to the Kensington Gardens.

If you think he was the only baby who ever wanted to escape, it shows how completely you have forgotten your own young days. When David heard this story first he was quite certain that he had never tried to escape, but I told him to think back hard, pressing his hands to his temples, and when he had done this hard, and even harder, he distinctly remembered a youthful desire to return to the tree-tops, and with that memory came others, as that he had lain in bed planning to escape as soon as his mother was asleep, and how she had once caught him half-way up the chimney. All children could have such recollections if they would press their hands hard to their temples, for, having been birds before they were human, they are naturally a little wild during the first few weeks, and very itchy at the shoulders, where their wings used to be. So David tells me.

I ought to mention here that the following is our way with a story: First I tell it to him, and then he tells it to me, the understanding being that it is quite a different story; and then I retell it with his additions, and so we go on until no one could say whether it is more his story or mine. In this story of Peter Pan, for instance, the bald narrative and most of the moral reflections are mine, though not all, for this boy can be a stern moralist; but the interesting bits about the ways and customs of babies in the bird-stage are mostly reminiscences of David's, recalled by pressing his hands to his temples and thinking hard.

Well, Peter Pan got out by the window, which had no bars. Standing on the ledge he could see trees far away, which were doubtless the Kensington Gardens, and the moment he saw them he entirely forgot that he was now a little boy in a nightgown, and away he flew, right over the houses to the Gardens. It is wonderful that he could fly without wings, but the place itched tremendously, and—and—perhaps we could all fly if we were as dead-confident-sure of our capacity to do it as was bold Peter Pan that evening.

He alighted gaily on the open sward, between the Baby's Palace and the Serpentine, and the first thing he did was to lie on his back and kick. He was quite unaware already that he had ever been human, and thought he was a bird, even in appearance, just the same as in his early days, and when he tried to

Away he flew, right over the houses to the Gardens.
[See page 31.]

catch a fly he did not understand that the reason he missed it was because he had attempted to seize it with his hand, which, of course, a bird never does. He saw, however, that it must be past Lock-out Time, for there were a good many fairies about, all too busy to notice him; they were getting breakfast ready, milking their cows, drawing water, and so on, and the sight of the water-pails made him thirsty, so he flew over to the Round Pond to have a drink. He stooped, and dipped his beak in the pond; he thought it was his beak, but, of course, it was only his nose, and therefore, very little water came up, and that not so refreshing as usual, so next he tried a puddle, and he fell flop into it. When a real bird falls in flop, he spreads out his feathers and pecks them dry, but Peter could not remember what was the thing to do, and he decided rather sulkily to go to sleep on the weeping-beech in the Baby Walk.

At first he found some difficulty in

balancing himself on a branch, but presently he remembered the way, and fell asleep. He awoke long before morning, shivering, and saying to himself, "I never was out on such a cold night"; he had really been out on colder nights when he was a bird, but, of course, as everybody knows, what seems a warm night to a bird is a cold night to a boy in a night-gown. Peter also felt strangely uncomfortable, as if his head was stuffy; he heard loud noises that made him look round sharply, though they were really himself sneezing. There was something he wanted very much, but, though he knew he wanted it, he could not think what it was. What he wanted so much was his mother to blow his nose, but that never struck him, so he decided to appeal to the fairies for enlightenment. They are reputed to know a good deal.

There were two of them strolling along the Baby Walk, with their arms round each other's waists, and he hopped down to address

The fairies have their tiffs with the birds.
[See page 36.]

them. The fairies have their tiffs with the birds, but they usually give a civil answer to a civil question, and he was quite angry when these two ran away the moment they saw him. Another was lolling on a garden chair, reading a postage-stamp which some human had let fall, and when he heard Peter's voice he popped in alarm behind a tulip.

To Peter's bewilderment he discovered that every fairy he met fled from him. A band of workmen, who were sawing down a toad-stool, rushed away, leaving their tools behind them. A milkmaid turned her pail upside down and hid in it. Soon the Gardens were in an uproar. Crowds of fairies were running this way and that, asking each other stoutly who was afraid; lights were extinguished, doors barricaded, and from the grounds of Queen Mab's palace came the rub-a-dub of drums, showing that the royal guard had been called out. A regiment of Lancers came charging down the Broad Walk, armed with

When he heard Peter's voice he popped in alarm behind a tulip.
[See page 36.]

A band of workmen, who were sawing down a toadstool, rushed away, leaving their tools behind them.
[See page 36.]

holly-leaves, with which they jag the enemy horribly in passing. Peter heard the little people crying everywhere that there was a human in the Gardens after Lock-out Time, but he never thought for a moment that he was the human. He was feeling stuffier and stuffier, and more and more wistful to learn what he wanted done to his nose, but he pursued them with the vital question in vain; the timid creatures ran from him, and even the Lancers, when he approached them up the Hump, turned swiftly into a side-walk, on the pretence that they saw him there.

Despairing of the fairies, he resolved to consult the birds, but now he remembered, as an odd thing, that all the birds on the weeping-beech had flown away when he alighted on it, and though this had not troubled him at the time, he saw its meaning now. Every living thing was shunning him. Poor little Peter Pan! he sat down and cried, and even then he did not know that, for a bird, he was sitting on his wrong part. It is a blessing that he did not know, for otherwise he would have lost faith in his power to fly, and the moment you doubt whether you can fly, you cease for ever to be able to do it. The reason birds can fly and we can't is simply that they have perfect faith, for to have faith is to have wings.

Now, except by flying, no one can reach the island in the Serpentine, for the boats of humans are forbidden to land there, and there are stakes round it, standing up in the water, on each of which a bird-sentinel sits by day and night. It was to the island that Peter now flew to put his strange case before old Solomon Caw, and he alighted on it with relief, much heartened to find himself at last at home, as the birds call the island. All of them were asleep, including the sentinels, except Solomon, who was wide awake on one side, and he listened quietly to Peter's adventures, and then told him their true meaning.

"Look at your nightgown, if you don't

Peter put his strange case before old Solomon Caw.
[See page 40.]

believe me," Solomon said; and with staring eyes Peter looked at his nightgown, and then at the sleeping birds. Not one of them wore anything.

"How many of your toes are thumbs?" said Solomon a little cruelly, and Peter saw to his consternation, that all his toes were fingers. The shock was so great that it drove away his cold.

"Ruffle your feathers," said that grim old Solomon, and Peter tried most desperately hard to ruffle his feathers, but he had none. Then he rose up, quaking, and for the first time since he stood on the window ledge, he remembered a lady who had been very fond of him.

"I think I shall go back to mother," he said timidly.

"Good-bye," replied Solomon Caw with a queer look.

But Peter hesitated. "Why don't you go?" the old one asked politely.

"I suppose," said Peter huskily, "I suppose I can still fly?"

You see he had lost faith.

"Poor little half-and-half!" said Solomon, who was not really hard-hearted, "you will never be able to fly again, not even on windy days. You must live here on the island always."

"And never even go to the Kensington Gardens?" Peter asked tragically.

"How could you get across?" said Solomon. He promised very kindly, however, to teach Peter as many of the bird ways as could be learned by one of such an awkward shape.

"Then I shan't be exactly a human?" Peter asked.

"No."

"Nor exactly a bird?"

"No."

"What shall I be?"

"You will be a Betwixt-and-Between,"

Solomon said, and certainly he was a wise old fellow, for that is exactly how it turned out.

The birds on the island never got used to him. His oddities tickled them every day, as if they were quite new, though it was really the birds that were new. They came out of the eggs daily, and laughed at him at once; then off they soon flew to be humans, and other birds came out of other eggs, and so it went on forever. The crafty mother-birds, when they tired of sitting on their eggs; used to get the young ones to break their shells a day before the right time by whispering to them that now was their chance to see Peter washing or drinking or eating. Thousands gathered round him daily to watch him do these things, just as you watch the peacocks, and they screamed with delight when he lifted the crusts they flung him with his hands instead of in the usual way with the mouth. All his food was brought to him from the Gardens at Solomon's orders by the birds. He would not eat worms or insects (which they thought very silly of him), so they brought him bread in their beaks. Thus, when you cry out, "Greedy! Greedy!" to the bird that flies away with the big crust, you know now that you ought not to do this, for he is very likely taking it to Peter Pan.

Peter wore no nightgown now. You see, the birds were always begging him for bits of it to line their nests with, and, being very good-natured, he could not refuse, so by Solomon's advice he had hidden what was left of it. But, though he was now quite naked, you must not think that he was cold or unhappy. He was usually very happy and gay, and the reason was that Solomon had kept his promise and taught him many of the bird ways. To be easily pleased, for instance, and always to be really doing something, and to think that whatever he was doing was a thing of vast importance. Peter became very clever at helping the birds to build their nests; soon he could build better than a wood-pigeon, and nearly as well as a blackbird, though never did he satisfy the finches, and he made nice little water-troughs near the nests and dug up worms for the young ones with his fingers. He also became very learned in bird-lore, and knew an east wind from a west wind by its smell, and he could see the grass growing and hear the insects walking about inside the tree-trunks. But the best thing Solomon had done was to teach him to have a glad heart. All birds have glad hearts unless you rob their nests, and so as they were the only kind of heart Solomon knew about, it was easy to him to teach Peter how to have one.

Peter's heart was so glad that he felt he must sing all day long, just as the birds sing for joy, but, being partly human, he needed an instrument, so he made a pipe of reeds, and he used to sit by the shore of the island of an evening, practising the sough of the wind and the ripple of the water, and catching handfuls of the shine of the moon, and he put them all in his pipe and played them so beautifully that even the birds were deceived, and they would say to each other, "Was that a fish leaping in the water or was it Peter playing leaping fish on his pipe?" And sometimes he played the birth of birds, and then the mothers would turn round in their nests to see whether they had laid an egg. If you are a child of the Gardens you must know the chestnut-tree near the bridge, which comes out in flower first of all the chestnuts, but perhaps you have not heard why this tree leads the way. It is because Peter wearies for summer and plays that it has come, and the chestnut being so near, hears him and is cheated.

But as Peter sat by the shore tootling divinely on his pipe he sometimes fell into sad thoughts, and then the music became sad also, and the reason of all this sadness was that he could not reach the Gardens, though he could see them through the arch of the bridge. He knew he could never be a real human again, and scarcely wanted to be one, but oh! how he longed to play as other children play, and of course there is no such lovely place to play in as the Gardens. The birds brought him news of how boys and girls play, and wistful tears started in Peter's eyes.

Perhaps you wonder why he did not swim across. The reason was that he could not swim. He wanted to know how to swim, but no one on the island knew the way except the ducks, and they are so stupid. They were quite willing to teach him, but all they could say about it was, "You sit down on the top of the water in this way, and then you kick out like that." Peter tried it often, but always before he could kick out he sank. What he really needed to know was how you sit on the water without sinking, and they said it was quite impossible to explain such an easy thing as that. Occasionally swans touched on the island, and he would give them all his day's food and then ask them how they sat on the water, but as soon as he had no more to give them the hateful things hissed at him and sailed away.

Once he really thought he had discovered a way of reaching the Gardens. A wonderful white thing, like a runaway newspaper, floated high over the island and then tumbled, rolling over and over after the manner of a bird that has broken its wing. Peter was so frightened that he hid, but the birds told him it was only a kite, and what a kite is, and that it must have tugged its string out of a boy's hand, and soared away. After that they laughed at Peter for being so fond of the kite; he loved it so much that he even slept with one hand on it, and I think this was pathetic and pretty, for the reason he loved it was because it had belonged to a real boy.

To the birds this was a very poor reason, but the older ones felt grateful to him at this time because he had nursed a number of fledglings through the German measles, and they offered to show him how birds fly a kite. So six of them took the end of the string in their beaks and flew away with it; and to his amazement it flew after them and went even higher than they.

Peter screamed out, "Do it again!" and with great good nature they did it several times, and always instead of thanking them he cried, "Do it again!" which shows that even now he had not quite forgotten what it was to be a boy.

At last, with a grand design burning within his brave heart, he begged them to do it once more with him clinging to the tail, and now a hundred flew off with the string, and Peter clung to the tail, meaning to drop off when he was over the Gardens. But the kite broke to pieces in the air, and he would have been drowned in the Serpentine had he not caught hold of two indignant swans and made them carry him to the island. After this the

Peter screamed out "Do it again!" and with great good-nature they did it several times.

[See page 50.]

A hundred flew off with the string, and Peter clung to the tail.
[See page 50.]

birds said that they would help him no more in his mad enterprise.

Nevertheless, Peter did reach the Gardens at last by the help of Shelley's boat, as I am now to tell you.

After this the birds said that they would help him no more in his mad enterprise.
[See page 50.]

III
The Thrush's Nest

SHELLEY was a young gentleman and as grown-up as he need ever expect to be. He was a poet; and they are never exactly grown-up. They are people who despise money except what you need for to-day, and he had all that and five pounds over. So, when he was walking in the Kensington Gardens, he made a paper boat of his bank-note, and sent it sailing on the Serpentine.

It reached the island at night; and the look-out brought it to Solomon Caw, who thought at first that it was the usual thing, a message from a lady, saying she would be obliged if he could let her have a good one. They always ask for the best one he has, and if he likes the letter he sends one from Class A, but if it ruffles him he sends very funny ones indeed. Sometimes he sends none at all, and at another time he sends a nestful; it all depends on the mood you catch him in. He likes you to leave it all to him, and if you mention particularly that you hope he will see his way to making it *a boy this time,* he is almost sure to send another girl. And whether you are a lady or only a little boy who wants a baby-sister, always take pains to write your address clearly. You can't think what a lot of babies Solomon has sent to the wrong house.

Shelley's boat, when opened, completely puzzled Solomon, and he took counsel of his assistants, who having walked over it twice, first with their toes pointed out, and then with their toes pointed in, decided that it came from some greedy person who wanted five. They thought this because there was a large five printed on it. "Preposterous!" cried Solomon in a rage, and he presented it to Peter; anything useless which drifted upon the island was usually given to Peter as a plaything.

"Preposterous!" cried Solomon in a rage.
[See page 56.]

But he did not play with his precious bank-note, for he knew what it was at once, having been very observant during the week when he was an ordinary boy. With so much money, he reflected, he could surely at last contrive to reach the Gardens, and he considered all the possible ways, and decided (wisely, I think) to choose the best way. But, first, he had to tell the birds of the value of Shelley's boat; and though they were too honest to demand it back, he saw that they were galled, and they cast such black looks at Solomon, who was rather vain of his cleverness, that he flew away to the end of the island, and sat there very depressed with his head buried in his wings. Now Peter knew that unless Solomon was on your side, you never got anything done for you in the island, so he followed him and tried to hearten him.

Nor was this all that Peter did to gain the powerful old fellow's good-will. You must know that Solomon had no intention of remaining in office all his life. He looked forward to retiring by and by, and devoting his green old age to a life of pleasure on a certain yew-stump in the Figs which had taken his fancy, and for years he had been quietly filling his stocking. It was a stocking belonging to some bathing person which had been cast upon the island, and at the time I speak of it contained a hundred and eighty crumbs, thirty-four nuts, sixteen crusts, a pen-wiper and a boot-lace. When his stocking was full, Solomon calculated that he would be able to retire on a competency. Peter now gave him a pound. He cut it off his bank-note with a sharp stick.

This made Solomon his friend for ever, and after the two had consulted together they called a meeting of the thrushes. You will see presently why thrushes only were invited.

The scheme to be put before them was really Peter's, but Solomon did most of the talking, because he soon became irritable if

For years he had been quietly filling his stocking.
[See page 59.]

other people talked. He began by saying that he had been much impressed by the superior ingenuity shown by the thrushes in nest-building, and this put them into good-humour at once, as it was meant to do; for all the quarrels between birds are about the best way of building nests. Other birds, said Solomon, omitted to line their nests with mud, and as a result they did not hold water. Here he cocked his head as if he had used an unanswerable argument; but, unfortunately, a Mrs. Finch had come to the meeting uninvited, and she squeaked out, "We don't build nests to hold water, but to hold eggs," and then the thrushes stopped cheering, and Solomon was so perplexed that he took several sips of water.

"Consider," he said at last, "how warm the mud makes the nest."

"Consider," cried Mrs. Finch, "that when water gets into the nest it remains there and your little ones are drowned."

The thrushes begged Solomon with a look

to say something crushing in reply to this, but again he was perplexed.

"Try another drink," suggested Mrs. Finch pertly. Kate was her name, and all Kates are saucy.

Solomon did try another drink, and it inspired him. "If," said he, "a finch's nest is placed on the Serpentine it fills and breaks to pieces, but a thrush's nest is still as dry as the cup of a swan's back."

How the thrushes applauded! Now they knew why they lined their nests with mud, and when Mrs. Finch called out, "We don't place our nests on the Serpentine," they did what they should have done at first—chased her from the meeting. After this it was most orderly. What they had been brought together to hear, said Solomon, was this: their young friend, Peter Pan, as they well knew, wanted very much to be able to cross to the Gardens, and he now proposed, with their help, to build a boat.

At this the thrushes began to fidget, which made Peter tremble for his scheme.

Solomon explained hastily that what he meant was not one of the cumbrous boats that humans use; the proposed boat was to be simply a thrush's nest large enough to hold Peter.

But still, to Peter's agony, the thrushes were sulky. "We are very busy people," they grumbled, "and this would be a big job."

"Quite so," said Solomon, "and, of course, Peter would not allow you to work for nothing. You must remember that he is now in comfortable circumstances, and he will pay you such wages as you have never been paid before. Peter Pan authorises me to say that you shall all be paid sixpence a day."

Then all the thrushes hopped for joy, and that very day was begun the celebrated Building of the Boat. All their ordinary business fell into arrears. It was the time of the year when they should have been pairing, but not a thrush's nest was built except this big one, and so Solomon soon ran short of thrushes with which to supply the demand from the mainland. The stout, rather greedy children, who look so well in perambulators but get puffed easily when they walk, were all young thrushes once, and ladies often ask specially for them. What do you think Solomon did? He sent over to the housetops for a lot of sparrows and ordered them to lay their eggs in old thrushes' nests, and sent their young to the ladies and swore they were all thrushes! It was known afterward on the island as the Sparrow's Year; and so, when you meet grown-up people in the Gardens who puff and blow as if they thought themselves bigger than they are, very likely they belong to that year. You ask them.

Peter was a just master, and paid his workpeople every evening. They stood in rows on the branches, waiting politely while he cut the paper sixpences out of his bank-note, and presently he called the roll, and then

When you meet grown-up people in the Gardens who puff and blow as if they thought themselves bigger than they are.
[See page 64.]

each bird, as the names were mentioned, flew down and got sixpence. It must have been a fine sight.

And at last, after months of labour, the boat was finished. O the glory of Peter as he saw it growing more and more like a great thrush's nest! From the very beginning of the building of it he slept by its side, and often woke up to say sweet things to it, and after it was lined with mud and the mud had dried he always slept in it. He sleeps in his nest still, and has a fascinating way of curling round in it, for it is just large enough to hold him comfortably when he curls round like a kitten. It is brown inside, of course, but outside it is mostly green, being woven of grass and twigs, and when these wither or snap the walls are thatched afresh. There are also a few feathers here and there, which came off the thrushes while they were building.

The other birds were extremely jealous, and said that the boat would not balance on the water, but it lay most beautifully steady; they said the water would come into it, but no water came into it. Next they said that Peter had no oars, and this caused the thrushes to look at each other in dismay; but Peter replied that he had no need of oars, for he had a sail, and with such a proud, happy face he produced a sail which he had fashioned out of his nightgown, and though it was still rather like a nightgown it made a lovely sail. And that night, the moon being full, and all the birds asleep, he did enter his coracle (as Master Francis Pretty would have said) and depart out of the island. And first, he knew not why, he looked upward, with his hands clasped, and from that moment his eyes were pinned to the west.

He had promised the thrushes to begin by making short voyages, with them as his guides, but far away he saw the Kensington Gardens beckoning to him beneath the bridge, and he could not wait. His face was flushed, but he never looked back; there was an exultation in his little breast that drove out fear. Was Peter the least gallant of the English mariners who have sailed westward to meet the Unknown?

At first, his boat turned round and round, and he was driven back to the place of his starting, whereupon he shortened sail, by removing one of the sleeves, and was forthwith carried backwards by a contrary breeze, to his no small peril. He now let go the sail, with the result that he was drifted toward the far shore, where are black shadows he knew not the dangers of, but suspected them, and so once more hoisted his nightgown and went roomer of the shadows until he caught a favouring wind, which bore him westward, but at so great a speed that he was like to be broke against the bridge. Which, having avoided, he passed under the bridge and came, to his great rejoicing, within full sight of the delectable Gardens. But having tried to cast

He passed under the bridge and came, to his great rejoicing, within full sight of the delectable Gardens.
[See page 68.]

anchor, which was a stone at the end of a piece of the kite-string, he found no bottom, and was fain to hold off, seeking for moorage; and, feeling his way, he buffeted against a sunken reef that cast him overboard by the greatness of the shock, and he was near to being drowned, but clambered back into the vessel. There now arose a mighty storm, accompanied by roaring of waters, such as he had never heard the like, and he was tossed this way and that, and his hands so numbed with the cold that he could not close them. Having escaped the danger of which, he was mercifully carried into a small bay, where his boat rode at peace.

Nevertheless, he was not yet in safety; for, on pretending to disembark, he found a multitude of small people drawn up on the shore to contest his landing, and shouting shrilly to him to be off, for it was long past Lock-out Time. This, with much brandishing of their holly-leaves; and also a company of them carried an arrow which some boy had left in the Gardens, and this they were prepared to use as a battering-ram.

Then Peter, who knew them for the fairies, called out that he was not an ordinary human and had no desire to do them displeasure, but to be their friend; nevertheless, having found a jolly harbour, he was in no temper to draw off therefrom, and he warned them if they sought to mischief him to stand to their harms.

So saying, he boldly leapt ashore, and they gathered around him with intent to slay him, but there then arose a great cry among the women, and it was because they had now observed that his sail was a baby's nightgown. Whereupon, they straightway loved him, and grieved that their laps were too small, the which I cannot explain, except by saying that such is the way of women. The men-fairies now sheathed their weapons on observing the behaviour of their women, on whose intelligence they set great store, and they led him civilly to their queen, who conferred upon him the courtesy of the Gardens after Lock-out Time, and henceforth Peter could go whither he chose, and the fairies had orders to put him in comfort.

Such was his first voyage to the Gardens, and you may gather from the antiquity of the language that it took place a long time ago. But Peter never grows any older, and if we could be watching for him under the bridge to-night (but, of course, we can't), I dare say we should see him hoisting his nightgown and sailing or paddling towards us in the Thrush's Nest. When he sails, he sits down, but he stands up to paddle. I shall tell you presently how he got his paddle.

Long before the time for the opening of the gates comes he steals back to the island, for people must not see him (he is not so human as all that), but this gives him hours for play, and he plays exactly as real children play. At least he thinks so, and it is one of the pathetic things about him that he often plays quite wrongly.

You see, he had no one to tell him how children really play, for the fairies were all more or less in hiding until dusk, and so know nothing, and though the birds pretended that they could tell him a great deal, when the time for telling came, it was wonderful how little they really knew. They told him the truth about hide-and-seek, and he often plays it by himself, but even the ducks on the Round Pond could not explain to him what it is that makes the pond so fascinating to boys. Every night the ducks have forgotten all the events of the day, except the number of pieces of cake thrown to them. They are gloomy creatures, and say that cake is not what it was in their young days.

So Peter had to find out many things for himself. He often played ships at the Round Pond, but his ship was only a hoop which he

Fairies are all more or less in hiding until dusk.
[See page 73.]

had found on the grass. Of course, he had never seen a hoop, and he wondered what you play at with them, and decided that you play at pretending they are boats. This hoop always sank at once, but he waded in for it, and sometimes he dragged it gleefully round the rim of the pond, and he was quite proud to think that he had discovered what boys do with hoops.

Another time, when he found a child's pail, he thought it was for sitting in, and he sat so hard in it that he could scarcely get out of it. Also he found a balloon. It was bobbing about on the Hump, quite as if it was having a game by itself, and he caught it after an exciting chase. But he thought it was a ball, and Jenny Wren had told him that boys kick balls, so he kicked it; and after that he could not find it anywhere.

Perhaps the most surprising thing he found was a perambulator. It was under a lime-tree, near the entrance to the Fairy

Queen's Winter Palace (which is within the circle of the seven Spanish chestnuts), and Peter approached it warily, for the birds had never mentioned such things to him. Lest it was alive, he addressed it politely; and then, as it gave no answer, he went nearer and felt it cautiously. He gave it a little push, and it ran from him, which made him think it must be alive after all; but, as it had run from him, he was not afraid. So he stretched out his hand to pull it to him, but this time it ran at him, and he was so alarmed that he leapt the railing and scudded away to his boat. You must not think, however, that he was a coward, for he came back next night with a crust in one hand and a stick in the other, but the perambulator had gone, and he never saw any other one. I have promised to tell you also about his paddle. It was a child's spade which he had found near St. Govor's Well, and he thought it was a paddle.

Do you pity Peter Pan for making these

mistakes? If so, I think it rather silly of you. What I mean is that, of course, one must pity him now and then, but to pity him all the time would be impertinence. He thought he had the most splendid time in the Gardens, and to think you have it is almost quite as good as really to have it. He played without ceasing, while you often waste time by being mad-dog or Mary-Annish. He could be neither of these things, for he had never heard of them, but do you think he is to be pitied for that?

Oh, he was merry! He was as much merrier than you, for instance, as you are merrier than your father. Sometimes he fell, like a spinning-top, from sheer merriment. Have you seen a greyhound leaping the fences of the Gardens? That is how Peter leaps them.

And think of the music of his pipe. Gentlemen who walk home at night write to the papers to say they heard a nightingale in the Gardens, but it is really Peter's pipe they hear. Of course, he had no mother—at least, what use was she to him? You can be sorry for him for that, but don't be too sorry, for the next thing I mean to tell you is how he revisited her. It was the fairies who gave him the chance.

IV
Lock-out Time

It is frightfully difficult to know much about the fairies, and almost the only thing known for certain is that there are fairies wherever there are children. Long ago children were forbidden the Gardens, and at that time there was not a fairy in the place; then the children were admitted, and the fairies came trooping in that very evening. They can't resist following the children, but you seldom see them, partly because they live in the daytime behind the railings, where you are not allowed to go, and also partly because they are so cunning. They are not a bit cunning after Lock-out, but until Lock-out, my word!

When you were a bird you knew the fairies pretty well, and you remember a good deal about them in your babyhood, which it is a great pity you can't write down, for gradually you forget, and I have heard of children who declared that they had never once seen a fairy. Very likely if they said this in the Kensington Gardens, they were standing looking at a fairy all the time. The reason they were cheated was that she pretended to be something else. This is one of their best tricks. They usually pretend to be flowers, because the court sits in the Fairies' Basin, and there are so many flowers there, and all along the Baby Walk, that a flower is the thing least likely to attract attention. They dress exactly like flowers, and change with the seasons, putting on white when lilies are in and blue for bluebells, and so on. They like crocus and hyacinth time best of all, as they are partial to a bit of colour, but tulips (except white ones, which are the fairy cradles) they consider garish, and they sometimes put off dressing like tulips for days, so that the beginning of the tulip weeks is almost the best time to catch them.

When they think you are not looking they skip along pretty lively, but if you look, and they fear there is no time to hide, they stand quite still pretending to be flowers. Then, after you have passed without knowing that they were fairies, they rush home and tell their mothers they have had such an adventure. The Fairy Basin, you remember, is all covered with ground-ivy (from which they make their castor-oil), with flowers growing in it here and there. Most of them really are flowers, but some of them are fairies. You never can be sure of them, but a good plan is to walk by looking the other way, and then turn round sharply. Another good plan, which David and I sometimes follow, is to stare them down. After a long time they can't help winking, and then you know for certain that they are fairies.

There are also numbers of them along the Baby Walk, which is a famous gentle place, as spots frequented by fairies are called. Once

When they think you are not looking they skip along pretty lively.
[See page 81.]

But if you look, and they fear there is no time to hide, they stand quite still pretending to be flowers.
[See page 81.]

twenty-four of them had an extraordinary adventure. They were a girls' school out for a walk with the governess, and all wearing hyacinth gowns, when she suddenly put her finger to her mouth, and then they all stood still on an empty bed and pretended to be hyacinths. Unfortunately what the governess had heard was two gardeners coming to plant new flowers in that very bed. They were wheeling a handcart with flowers in it, and were quite surprised to find the bed occupied. "Pity to lift them hyacinths," said the one man. "Duke's orders," replied the other, and, having emptied the cart, they dug up the boarding-school and put the poor, terrified things in it in five rows. Of course, neither the governess nor the girls dare let on that they were fairies, so they were carted far away to a potting-shed, out of which they escaped in the night without their shoes, but there was a great row about it among the parents, and the school was ruined.

As for their houses, it is no use looking for them, because they are the exact opposite of our houses. You can see our houses by day but you can't see them by dark. Well, you can see their houses by dark, but you can't see them by day, for they are the colour of night, and I never heard of any one yet who could see night in the daytime. This does not mean that they are black, for night has its colours just as day has, but ever so much brighter. Their blues and reds and greens are like ours with a light behind them. The palace is entirely built of many-coloured glasses, and is quite the loveliest of all royal residences, but the queen sometimes complains because the common people will peep in to see what she is doing. They are very inquisitive folk, and press quite hard against the glass, and that is why their noses are mostly snubby. The streets are miles long and very twisty, and have paths on each side made of bright worsted. The birds used to steal the worsted for their nests, but a policeman has been appointed to hold on at the other end.

One of the great differences between the fairies and us is that they never do anything useful. When the first baby laughed for the first time, his laugh broke into a million pieces, and they all went skipping about. That was the beginning of fairies. They look tremendously busy, you know, as if they had not a moment to spare, but if you were to ask them what they are doing, they could not tell you in the least. They are frightfully ignorant, and everything they do is make-believe. They have a postman, but he never calls except at Christmas with his little box, and though they have beautiful schools, nothing is taught in them; the youngest child being chief person is always elected mistress, and when she has called the roll, they all go out for a walk and never come back. It is a very noticeable thing that, in fairy families, the youngest is always chief person, and usually becomes a prince or princess; and children remember this, and think it must be so among humans also, and that is why they are often made uneasy when they come upon their mother furtively putting new frills on the basinette.

You have probably observed that your baby-sister wants to do all sorts of things that your mother and her nurse want her not to do—to stand up at sitting-down time, and to sit down at stand-up time, for instance, or to wake up when she should fall asleep, or to crawl on the floor when she is wearing her best frock, and so on, and perhaps you put this down to naughtiness. But it is not; it simply means that she is doing as she has seen the fairies do; she begins by following their ways, and it takes about two years to get her into the human ways. Her fits of passion, which are awful to behold, and are usually called teething, are no such thing; they are her natural exasperation, because we don't understand her, though she is talking an intelligible language. She is talking fairy. The reason mothers and nurses know what her remarks mean, before other people know, as that "Guch" means "Give it to me at once," while "Wa" is "Why do you wear such a funny hat?" is because, mixing so much with babies, they have picked up a little of the fairy language.

Of late David has been thinking back hard about the fairy tongue, with his hands clutching his temples, and he has remembered a number of their phrases which I shall tell you some day if I don't forget. He had heard them in the days when he was a thrush, and though I suggested to him that perhaps it is really bird language he is remembering, he says not, for these phrases are about fun and adventures, and the birds talked of nothing but nest-building. He distinctly remembers that the birds used to go from spot to spot like ladies at shop windows, looking at the different nests and saying, "Not my colour, my dear," and "How would that do with a soft lining?" and "But will it wear?" and "What hideous trimming!" and so on.

The fairies are exquisite dancers, and that is why one of the first things the baby does is to sign to you to dance to him and then to cry when you do it. They hold their great balls in the open air, in what is called a fairy ring. For weeks afterwards you can see the ring on the grass. It is not there when they begin, but they make it by waltzing round and round. Sometimes you will find mushrooms inside the ring, and these are fairy chairs that the servants have forgotten to clear away. The chairs and the rings are the only tell-tale marks these little people leave behind them, and they would remove even these were they not so fond of dancing that they toe it till the very moment of the opening of the gates. David and I once found a fairy ring quite warm.

But there is also a way of finding out

The fairies are exquisite dancers.
[See page 89.]

about the ball before it takes place. You know the boards which tell at what time the Gardens are to close to-day. Well, these tricky fairies sometimes slyly change the board on a ball night, so that it says the Gardens are to close at six-thirty, for instance, instead of at seven. This enables them to get begun half an hour earlier.

If on such a night we could remain behind in the Gardens, as the famous Maimie Mannering did, we might see delicious sights; hundreds of lovely fairies hastening to the ball, the married ones wearing their wedding rings round their waists; the gentlemen, all in uniform, holding up the ladies' trains, and linkmen running in front carrying winter cherries, which are the fairy-lanterns, the cloakroom where they put on their silver slippers and get a ticket for their wraps; the flowers streaming up from the Baby Walk to look on, and always welcome because they can lend a pin; the supper-table, with Queen Mab

These tricky fairies sometimes slyly change the board on a ball night.
[See page 91.]

Linkmen running in front carrying winter cherries.
[See page 91.]

at the head of it, and behind her chair the Lord Chamberlain, who carries a dandelion on which he blows when Her Majesty wants to know the time.

The table-cloth varies according to the seasons, and in May it is made of chestnut blossom. The way the fairy servants do is this: The men, scores of them, climb up the trees and shake the branches, and the blossom falls like snow. Then the lady servants sweep it together by whisking their skirts until it is exactly like a tablecloth, and that is how they get their tablecloth.

They have real glasses and real wine of three kinds, namely, blackthorn wine, berberris wine, and cowslip wine, and the Queen pours out, but the bottles are so heavy that she just pretends to pour out. There is bread-and-butter to begin with, of the size of a threepenny bit; and cakes to end with, and they are so small that they have no crumbs. The fairies sit round on mushrooms, and at first they are

When her Majesty wants to know the time.
[See page 94.]

The fairies sit round on mushrooms, and at first they are well-behaved.
[See page 94.]

well-behaved and always cough off the table, and so on, but after a bit they are not so well-behaved and stick their fingers into the butter, which is got from the roots of old trees, and the really horrid ones crawl over the table-cloth chasing sugar or other delicacies with their tongues. When the Queen sees them doing this she signs to the servants to wash up and put away, and then everybody adjourns to the dance, the Queen walking in front while the Lord Chamberlain walks behind her, carrying two little pots, one of which contains the juice of wallflower and the other the juice of Solomon's seals. Wallflower juice is good for reviving dancers who fall to the ground in a fit, and Solomon's seals juice is for bruises. They bruise very easily, and when Peter plays faster and faster they foot it till they fall down in fits. For, as you know without my telling you, Peter Pan is the fairies' orchestra. He sits in the middle of the ring, and they would never dream of having a smart dance

Butter is got from the roots of old trees.
[See page 97.]

Wallflower juice is good for reviving dancers
who fall to the ground in a fit.
[See page 97.]

nowadays without him. "P. P." is written on the corner of the invitation-cards sent out by all really good families. They are grateful little people, too, and at the princess's coming-of-age ball (they come of age on their second birthday and have a birthday every month) they gave him the wish of his heart.

The way it was done was this. The Queen ordered him to kneel, and then said that for playing so beautifully she would give him the wish of his heart. Then they all gathered round Peter to hear what was the wish of his heart, but for a long time he hesitated, not being certain what it was himself.

"If I chose to go back to mother," he asked at last, "could you give me that wish?"

Now this question vexed them, for were he to return to his mother they should lose his music, so the Queen tilted her nose contemptuously and said, "Pooh! ask for a much bigger wish than that."

"Is that quite a little wish?" he inquired.

Peter Pan is the fairies' orchestra.
[See page 97.]

"As little as this," the Queen answered, putting her hands near each other.

"What size is a big wish?" he asked.

She measured it off on her skirt and it was a very handsome length.

Then Peter reflected and said, "Well, then, I think I shall have two little wishes instead of one big one."

Of course, the fairies had to agree, though his cleverness rather shocked them, and he said that his first wish was to go to his mother, but with the right to return to the Gardens if he found her disappointing. His second wish he would hold in reserve.

They tried to dissuade him, and even put obstacles in the way.

"I can give you the power to fly to her house," the Queen said, "but I can't open the door for you."

"The window I flew out at will be open," Peter said confidently. "Mother always keeps it open in the hope that I may fly back."

"How do you know?" they asked, quite surprised, and, really, Peter could not explain how he knew.

"I just do know," he said.

So as he persisted in his wish, they had to grant it. The way they gave him power to fly was this: They all tickled him on the shoulder, and soon he felt a funny itching in that part, and then up he rose higher and higher, and flew away out of the Gardens and over the housetops.

It was so delicious that instead of flying straight to his old home he skimmed away over St. Paul's to the Crystal Palace and back by the river and Regent's Park, and by the time he reached his mother's window he had quite made up his mind that his second wish should be to become a bird.

The window was wide open, just as he knew it would be, and in he fluttered, and there was his mother lying asleep. Peter alighted softly on the wooden rail at the foot of

They all tickled him on the shoulder.
[See page 103.]

the bed and had a good look at her. She lay with her head on her hand, and the hollow in the pillow was like a nest lined with her brown wavy hair. He remembered, though he had long forgotten it, that she always gave her hair a holiday at night. How sweet the frills of her nightgown were. He was very glad she was such a pretty mother.

But she looked sad, and he knew why she looked sad. One of her arms moved as if it wanted to go round something, and he knew what it wanted to go round.

"O mother!" said Peter to himself, "if you just knew who is sitting on the rail at the foot of the bed."

Very gently he patted the little mound that her feet made, and he could see by her face that she liked it. He knew he had but to say "Mother" ever so softly, and she would wake up. They always wake up at once if it is you that says their name. Then she would give such a joyous cry and squeeze him tight. How nice that would be to him, but oh! how exquisitely delicious it would be to her. That, I am afraid, is how Peter regarded it. In returning to his mother he never doubted that he was giving her the greatest treat a woman can have. Nothing can be more splendid, he thought, than to have a little boy of your own. How proud of him they are! and very right and proper, too.

But why does Peter sit so long on the rail; why does he not tell his mother that he has come back?

I quite shrink from the truth, which is that he sat there in two minds. Sometimes he looked longingly at his mother, and sometimes he looked longingly at the window. Certainly it would be pleasant to be her boy again, but on the other hand, what times those had been in the Gardens! Was he so sure that he should enjoy wearing clothes again? He popped off the bed and opened some drawers to have a look at his old garments. They were still there, but he could not remember how you put them on. The socks, for instance, were they worn on the hands or on the feet? He was about to try one of them on his hand, when he had a great adventure. Perhaps the drawer had creaked; at any rate, his mother woke up, for he heard her say "Peter," as if it was the most lovely word in the language. He remained sitting on the floor and held his breath, wondering how she knew that he had come back. If she said "Peter" again, he meant to cry "Mother" and run to her. But she spoke no more, she made little moans only, and when he next peeped at her she was once more asleep, with tears on her face.

It made Peter very miserable, and what do you think was the first thing he did? Sitting on the rail at the foot of the bed, he played a beautiful lullaby to his mother on his pipe. He had made it up himself out of the way she said "Peter," and he never stopped playing until she looked happy.

He thought this so clever of him that he could scarcely resist wakening her to hear her say, "Oh, Peter, how exquisitely you play." However, as she now seemed comfortable, he again cast looks at the window. You must not think that he meditated flying away and never coming back. He had quite decided to be his mother's boy, but hesitated about beginning to-night. It was the second wish which troubled him. He no longer meant to make it a wish to be a bird, but not to ask for a second wish seemed wasteful, and, of course, he could not ask for it without returning to the fairies. Also, if he put off asking for his wish too long it might go bad. He asked himself if he had not been hard-hearted to fly away without saying good-bye to Solomon. "I should like awfully to sail in my boat just once more," he said wistfully to his sleeping mother. He quite argued with her as if she could hear him. "It would be so splendid to tell the birds of this adventure," he said coaxingly.

"I promise to come back," he said solemnly, and meant it, too.

And in the end, you know, he flew away. Twice he came back from the window, wanting to kiss his mother, but he feared the delight of it might waken her, so at last he played her a lovely kiss on his pipe, and then he flew back to the Gardens.

Many nights, and even months, passed before he asked the fairies for his second wish; and I am not sure that I quite know why he delayed so long. One reason was that he had so many good-byes to say, not only to his particular friends, but to a hundred favourite spots. Then he had his last sail, and his very last sail, and his last sail of all, and so on. Again, a number of farewell feasts were given in his honour; and another comfortable reason was that, after all, there was no hurry, for his mother would never weary of waiting for him. This last reason displeased old Solomon, for it was an encouragement to the birds to procrastinate. Solomon had several excellent mottoes for keeping them at their work, such as "Never put off laying to-day because you can lay to-morrow," and "In this world there are no second chances," and yet here was Peter gaily putting off and none the worse for it. The birds pointed this out to each other, and fell into lazy habits.

But, mind you, though Peter was so slow in going back to his mother, he was quite decided to go back. The best proof of this was his caution with the fairies. They were most anxious that he should remain in the Gardens to play to them, and to bring this to pass they tried to trick him into making such a remark as "I wish the grass was not so wet," and some of them danced out of time in the hope that he might cry, "I do wish you would keep time!" Then they would have said that this was his second wish. But he smoked their design, and though on occasions he began, "I wish——" he always stopped in time. So when at last he said to them bravely, "I wish now to go back to mother for ever and always," they had to tickle his shoulders and let him go.

He went in a hurry in the end, because he had dreamt that his mother was crying, and he knew what was the great thing she cried for, and that a hug from her splendid Peter would quickly make her to smile. Oh! he felt sure of it, and so eager was he to be nestling in her arms that this time he flew straight to the window, which was always to be open for him.

But the window was closed, and there were iron bars on it, and peering inside he saw his mother sleeping peacefully with her arm round another little boy.

Peter called, "Mother! mother!" but she heard him not; in vain he beat his little limbs against the iron bars. He had to fly back, sobbing, to the Gardens, and he never saw his dear again. What a glorious boy he had meant to be to her! Ah, Peter! we who have made the great mistake, how differently we should all act at the second chance. But Solomon was right—there is no second chance, not for most of us. When we reach the window it is Lock-out Time. The iron bars are up for life.

V
The Little House

Everybody has heard of the Little House in the Kensington Gardens, which is the only house in the whole world that the fairies have built for humans. But no one has really seen it, except just three or four, and they have not only seen it but slept in it, and unless you sleep in it you never see it. This is because it is not there when you lie down, but it is there when you wake up and step outside.

In a kind of way every one may see it, but what you see is not really it, but only the light in the windows. You see the light after Lock-out Time. David, for instance, saw it quite distinctly far away among the trees as we were going home from the pantomime, and Oliver Bailey saw it the night he stayed so late at the Temple, which is the name of his father's office. Angela Clare, who loves to have a tooth extracted because then she is treated to tea in a shop, saw more than one light, she saw hundreds of them all together; and this must have been the fairies building the house, for they build it every night, and always in a different part of the Gardens. She thought one of the lights was bigger than the others, though she was not quite sure, for they jumped about so, and it might have been another one that was bigger. But if it was the same one, it was Peter Pan's light. Heaps of children have seen the light, so that is nothing. But Maimie Mannering was the famous one for whom the house was first built.

Maimie was always rather a strange girl, and it was at night that she was strange. She was four years of age, and in the daytime she was the ordinary kind. She was pleased when her brother Tony, who was a magnificent fellow of six, took notice of her, and she looked up to him in the right way, and tried in vain to imitate him and was flattered rather than annoyed when he shoved her about. Also, when she was batting, she would pause though the ball was in the air to point out to you that she was wearing new shoes. She was quite the ordinary kind in the daytime.

But as the shades of night fell, Tony, the swaggerer, lost his contempt for Maimie and eyed her fearfully; and no wonder, for with dark there came into her face a look that I can describe only as a leary look. It was also a serene look that contrasted grandly with Tony's uneasy glances. Then he would make her presents of his favourite toys (which he always took away from her next morning), and she accepted them with a disturbing smile. The reason he was now become so wheedling and she so mysterious was (in brief) that they knew they were about to be sent to bed. It was then that Maimie was terrible. Tony entreated her not to do it to-night, and the mother and their coloured nurse threatened her, but Maimie merely smiled her agitating smile. And by and by when they were alone with their night-light she would start up in bed crying "Hsh! what was that?" Tony beseeches her, "It was nothing—don't, Maimie, don't!" and pulls the sheet over his head. "It is coming nearer!" she cries. "Oh, look at it, Tony! It is feeling your bed with its horns—it is boring for you, O Tony, oh!" and she desists not until he rushes downstairs in his combinations, screeching. When they came up to whip Maimie they usually found her sleeping tranquilly—not shamming, you know, but really sleeping, and looking like the sweetest little angel, which seems to me to make it almost worse.

But of course it was daytime when they were in the Gardens, and then Tony did most of the talking. You could gather from his talk that he was a very brave boy, and no one was so proud of it as Maimie. She would have loved to have a ticket on her saying that she was his sister. And at no time did she admire him more than when he told her, as he often did with splendid firmness, that one day he meant to remain behind in the Gardens after the gates were closed.

"Oh, Tony," she would say, with awful respect, "but the fairies will be so angry!"

"I daresay," replied Tony, carelessly.

"Perhaps," she said, thrilling, "Peter Pan will give you a sail in his boat!"

"I shall make him," replied Tony; no wonder she was proud of him.

But they should not have talked so loudly, for one day they were overheard by a fairy who had been gathering skeleton leaves, from which the little people weave their summer curtains, and after that Tony was a marked boy. They loosened the rails before he sat on them, so that down he came on the back of his head; they tripped him up by catching his bootlace, and bribed the ducks to sink his boat. Nearly all the nasty accidents you meet

One day they were overheard by a fairy.
[See page 117.]

The little people weave their summer curtains from skeleton leaves.
[See page 117.]

with in the Gardens occur because the fairies have taken an ill-will to you, and so it behoves you to be careful what you say about them.

Maimie was one of the kind who like to fix a day for doing things, but Tony was not that kind, and when she asked him which day he was to remain behind in the Gardens after Lock-out he merely replied, "Just some day"; he was quite vague about which day except when she asked, "Will it be to-day?" and then he could always say for certain that it would not be to-day. So she saw that he was waiting for a real good chance.

This brings us to an afternoon when the Gardens were white with snow, and there was ice on the Round Pond; not thick enough to skate on, but at least you could spoil it for to-morrow by flinging stones, and many bright little boys and girls were doing that.

When Tony and his sister arrived they wanted to go straight to the pond, but their ayah said they must take a sharp walk first,

An afternoon when the Gardens were white with snow.
[See page 120.]

and as she said this she glanced at the time-board to see when the Gardens closed that night. It read half-past five. Poor ayah! she is the one who laughs continuously because there are so many white children in the world, but she was not to laugh much more that day.

Well, they went up the Baby Walk and back, and when they returned to the time-board she was surprised to see that it now read five o'clock for closing-time. But she was unacquainted with the tricky ways of the fairies, and so did not see (as Maimie and Tony saw at once) that they had changed the hour because there was to be a ball to-night. She said there was only time now to walk to the top of the Hump and back, and as they trotted along with her she little guessed what was thrilling their little breasts. You see the chance had come of seeing a fairy ball. Never, Tony felt, could he hope for a better chance.

He had to feel this for Maimie so plainly felt it for him. Her eager eyes asked the question, "Is it to-day?" and he gasped and then nodded. Maimie slipped her hand into Tony's, and hers was hot, but his was cold. She did a very kind thing; she took off her scarf and gave it to him. "In case you should feel cold," she whispered. Her face was aglow, but Tony's was very gloomy.

As they turned on the top of the Hump he whispered to her, "I'm afraid nurse would see me, so I shan't be able to do it."

Maimie admired him more than ever for being afraid of nothing but their ayah, when there were so many unknown terrors to fear, and she said aloud, "Tony, I shall race you to the gate," and in a whisper, "Then you can hide," and off they ran.

Tony could always outdistance her easily, but never had she known him speed away so quickly as now, and she was sure he hurried that he might have more time to hide. "Brave, brave!" her doting eyes were crying when she got a dreadful shock; instead of hiding, her hero had run out at the gate! At this bitter sight Maimie stopped blankly, as if all her lapful of darling treasures were suddenly spilled, and then for very disdain she could not sob; in a swell of protest against all puling cowards she ran to St. Govor's Well and hid in Tony's stead.

When the ayah reached the gate and saw Tony far in front she thought her other charge was with him and passed out. Twilight crept over the Gardens, and hundreds of people passed out, including the last one, who always has to run for it, but Maimie saw them not. She had shut her eyes tight and glued them with passionate tears. When she opened them something very cold ran up her legs and up her arms and dropped into her heart. It was the stillness of the Gardens. Then she heard *clang,* then from another part *clang,* then *clang, clang* far away. It was the Closing of the Gates.

Immediately the last clang had died away Maimie distinctly heard a voice say, "So that's

She ran to St. Govor's Well and hid.
[See page 124.]

all right." It had a wooden sound and seemed to come from above, and she looked up in time to see an elm-tree stretching out its arms and yawning.

She was about to say, "I never knew you could speak!" when a metallic voice that seemed to come from the ladle at the well remarked to the elm, "I suppose it is a bit coldish up there?" and the elm replied, "Not particularly, but you do get numb standing so long on one leg," and he flapped his arms vigorously just as the cabmen do before they drive off. Maimie was quite surprised to see that a number of other tall trees were doing the same sort of thing, and she stole away to the Baby Walk and crouched observantly under a Minorca holly which shrugged its shoulders but did not seem to mind her.

She was not in the least cold. She was wearing a russet-coloured pelisse and had the hood over her head, so that nothing of her showed except her dear little face and her curls. The rest of her real self was hidden far away inside so many warm garments that in shape she seemed rather like a ball. She was about forty round the waist.

There was a good deal going on in the Baby Walk, when Maimie arrived in time to see a magnolia and a Persian lilac step over the railing and set off for a smart walk. They moved in a jerky sort of way certainly, but that was because they used crutches. An elderberry hobbled across the walk, and stood chatting with some young quinces, and they all had crutches. The crutches were the sticks that are tied to young trees and shrubs. They were quite familiar objects to Maimie, but she had never known what they were for until to-night.

She peeped up the walk and saw her first fairy. He was a street boy fairy who was running up the walk closing the weeping trees. The way he did it was this: he pressed a spring in the trunks and they shut like umbrellas,

An elderberry hobbled across the walk,
and stood chatting with some young quinces.
[See page 127.]

deluging the little plants beneath with snow. "O you naughty, naughty child!" Maimie cried indignantly, for she knew what it was to have a dripping umbrella about your ears.

Fortunately the mischievous fellow was out of earshot, but a chrysanthemum heard her, and said so pointedly, "Hoity-toity, what is this?" that she had to come out and show herself. Then the whole vegetable kingdom was rather puzzled what to do.

"Of course it is no affair of ours," a spindle-tree said after they had whispered together, "but you know quite well you ought not to be here, and perhaps our duty is to report you to the fairies; what do you think yourself?"

"I think you should not," Maimie replied, which so perplexed them that they said petulantly there was no arguing with her. "I wouldn't ask it of you," she assured them, "if I thought it was wrong," and of course after this they could not well carry tales. They then said,

A chrysanthemum heard her, and said so pointedly,
"Hoity-toity, what is this?"
[See page 129.]

"Well-a-day," and "Such is life," for they can be frightfully sarcastic; but she felt sorry for those of them who had no crutches, and she said good-naturedly, "Before I go to the fairies' ball, I should like to take you for a walk one at a time; you can lean on me, you know."

At this they clapped their hands, and she escorted them up the Baby Walk and back again, one at a time, putting an arm or a finger round the very frail, setting their leg right when it got too ridiculous, and treating the foreign ones quite as courteously as the English, though she could not understand a word they said.

They behaved well on the whole, though some whimpered that she had not taken them as far as she took Nancy or Grace or Dorothy, and others jagged her, but it was quite unintentional, and she was too much of a lady to cry out. So much walking tired her, and she was anxious to be off to the ball, but she no longer felt afraid. The reason she felt no more fear was that it was now night-time, and in the dark, you remember, Maimie was always rather strange.

They were now loth to let her go, for, "If the fairies see you," they warned her, "they will mischief you—stab you to death, or compel you to nurse their children, or turn you into something tedious, like an evergreen oak." As they said this they looked with affected pity at an evergreen oak, for in winter they are very envious of the evergreens.

"Oh, la!" replied the oak bitingly, "how deliciously cosy it is to stand here buttoned to the neck and watch you poor naked creatures shivering."

This made them sulky, though they had really brought it on themselves, and they drew for Maimie a very gloomy picture of the perils that faced her if she insisted on going to the ball.

She learned from a purple filbert that the court was not in its usual good temper at

They warned her.
[See page 132.]

present, the cause being the tantalising heart of the Duke of Christmas Daisies. He was an Oriental fairy, very poorly of a dreadful complaint, namely, inability to love, and though he had tried many ladies in many lands he could not fall in love with one of them. Queen Mab, who rules in the Gardens, had been confident that her girls would bewitch him, but alas! his heart, the doctor said, remained cold. This rather irritating doctor, who was his private physician, felt the Duke's heart immediately after any lady was presented, and then always shook his bald head and murmured, "Cold, quite cold." Naturally Queen Mab felt disgraced, and first she tried the effect of ordering the court into tears for nine minutes, and then she blamed the Cupids and decreed that they should wear fools' caps until they thawed the Duke's frozen heart.

"How I should love to see the Cupids in their dear little fools' caps!" Maimie cried, and away she ran to look for them very recklessly,

Queen Mab, who rules in the Gardens.
[See page 134.]

Shook his bald head and murmured, "Cold, quite cold."
[See page 134.]

for the Cupids hate to be laughed at.

It is always easy to discover where a fairies' ball is being held, as ribbons are stretched between it and all the populous parts of the Gardens, on which those invited may walk to the dance without wetting their pumps. This night the ribbons were red, and looked very pretty on the snow.

Maimie walked alongside one of them for some distance without meeting anybody, but at last she saw a fairy cavalcade approaching. To her surprise they seemed to be returning from the ball, and she had just time to hide from them by bending her knees and holding out her arms and pretending to be a garden chair. There were six horsemen in front and six behind; in the middle walked a prim lady wearing a long train held up by two pages, and on the train, as if it were a couch, reclined a lovely girl, for in this way do aristocratic fairies travel about. She was dressed in golden rain, but the most enviable part of her was her neck, which was blue in colour and of a velvet texture, and of course showed off her diamond necklace as no white throat could have glorified it. The high-born fairies obtain this admired effect by pricking their skin, which lets the blue blood come through and dye them, and you cannot imagine anything so dazzling unless you have seen the ladies' busts in the jewellers' windows.

Maimie also noticed that the whole cavalcade seemed to be in a passion, tilting their noses higher than it can be safe for even fairies to tilt them, and she concluded that this must be another case in which the doctor had said, "Cold, quite cold!"

Well, she followed the ribbon to a place where it became a bridge over a dry puddle into which another fairy had fallen and been unable to climb out. At first this little damsel was afraid of Maimie, who most kindly went to her aid, but soon she sat in her hand chatting gaily and explaining that her name was

Brownie, and that though only a poor street singer she was on her way to the ball to see if the Duke would have her.

"Of course," she said, "I am rather plain," and this made Maimie uncomfortable, for indeed the simple little creature was almost quite plain for a fairy.

It was difficult to know what to reply.

"I see you think I have no chance," Brownie said falteringly.

"I don't say that," Maimie answered politely; "of course your face is just a tiny bit homely, but——" Really it was quite awkward for her.

Fortunately she remembered about her father and the bazaar. He had gone to a fashionable bazaar where all the most beautiful ladies in London were on view for half a crown the second day, but on his return home, instead of being dissatisfied with Maimie's mother, he had said, "You can't think, my dear, what a relief it is to see a homely face again."

Maimie repeated this story, and it fortified Brownie tremendously, indeed she had no longer the slightest doubt that the Duke would choose her. So she scudded away up the ribbon, calling out to Maimie not to follow lest the Queen should mischief her.

But Maimie's curiosity tugged her forward, and presently at the seven Spanish chestnuts she saw a wonderful light. She crept forward until she was quite near it, and then she peeped from behind a tree.

The light, which was as high as your head above the ground, was composed of myriads of glow-worms all holding on to each other, and so forming a dazzling canopy over the fairy ring. There were thousands of little people looking on, but they were in shadow and drab in colour compared to the glorious creatures within that luminous circle, who were so bewilderingly bright that Maimie had to wink hard all the time she looked at them.

It was amazing and even irritating to her

that the Duke of Christmas Daisies should be able to keep out of love for a moment: yet out of love his dusky grace still was: you could see it by the shamed looks of the Queen and court (though they pretended not to care), by the way darling ladies brought forward for his approval burst into tears as they were told to pass on, and by his own most dreary face.

Maimie could also see the pompous doctor feeling the Duke's heart and hear him give utterance to his parrot cry, and she was particularly sorry for the Cupids, who stood in their fools' caps in obscure places and, every time they heard that "Cold, quite cold," bowed their disgraced little heads.

She was disappointed not to see Peter Pan, and I may as well tell you now why he was so late that night. It was because his boat had got wedged on the Serpentine between fields of floating ice, through which he had to break a perilous passage with his trusty paddle.

The fairies had as yet scarcely missed him, for they could not dance, so heavy were their hearts. They forget all the steps when they are sad, and remember them again when they are merry. David tells me that fairies never say "We feel happy": what they say is, "We feel *dancey*."

Well, they were looking very undancey indeed, when sudden laughter broke out among the onlookers, caused by Brownie, who had just arrived and was insisting on her right to be presented to the Duke.

Maimie craned forward eagerly to see how her friend fared, though she had really no hope; no one seemed to have the least hope except Brownie herself, who, however, was absolutely confident. She was led before his grace, and the doctor putting a finger carelessly on the ducal heart, which for convenience' sake was reached by a little trap-door in his diamond shirt, had begun to say mechanically, "Cold, qui—," when he stopped abruptly.

Fairies never say, "We feel happy": what they say is, "We feel dancey."
[See page 142.]

Looking very undancey indeed.
[See page 142.]

"What's this?" he cried, and first he shook the heart like a watch, and then put his ear to it.

"Bless my soul!" cried the doctor, and by this time of course the excitement among the spectators was tremendous, fairies fainting right and left.

Everybody stared breathlessly at the Duke, who was very much startled, and looked as if he would like to run away. "Good gracious me!" the doctor was heard muttering, and now the heart was evidently on fire, for he had to jerk his fingers away from it and put them in his mouth.

The suspense was awful.

Then in a loud voice, and bowing low, "My Lord Duke," said the physician elatedly, "I have the honour to inform your excellency that your grace is in love."

You can't conceive the effect of it. Brownie held out her arms to the Duke and he flung himself into them, the Queen leapt

"My Lord Duke," said the physician elatedly, "I have the honour to inform your excellency that your grace is in love."
[See page 145.]

into the arms of the Lord Chamberlain, and the ladies of the court leapt into the arms of her gentlemen, for it is etiquette to follow her example in everything. Thus in a single moment about fifty marriages took place, for if you leap into each other's arms it is a fairy wedding. Of course a clergyman has to be present.

How the crowd cheered and leapt! Trumpets brayed, the moon came out, and immediately a thousand couples seized hold of its rays as if they were ribbons in a May dance and waltzed in wild abandon round the fairy ring. Most gladsome sight of all, the Cupids plucked the hated fools' caps from their heads and cast them high in the air. And then Maimie went and spoiled everything.

She couldn't help it. She was crazy with delight over her little friend's good fortune, so she took several steps forward and cried in an ecstasy, "O Brownie, how splendid!"

Everybody stood still, the music ceased,

the lights went out, and all in the time you may take to say, "Oh dear!" An awful sense of her peril came upon Maimie; too late she remembered that she was a lost child in a place where no human must be between the locking and the opening of the gates; she heard the murmur of an angry multitude; she saw a thousand swords flashing for her blood, and she uttered a cry of terror and fled.

How she ran! and all the time her eyes were starting out of her head. Many times she lay down, and then quickly jumped up and ran on again. Her little mind was so entangled in terrors that she no longer knew she was in the Gardens. The one thing she was sure of was that she must never cease to run, and she thought she was still running long after she had dropped in the Figs and gone to sleep. She thought the snowflakes falling on her face were her mother kissing her good-night. She thought her coverlet of snow was a warm blanket, and tried to pull it over her head. And when she heard talking through her dreams she thought it was mother bringing father to the nursery door to look at her as she slept. But it was the fairies.

I am very glad to be able to say that they no longer desired to mischief her. When she rushed away they had rent the air with such cries as "Slay her!" "Turn her into something extremely unpleasant!" and so on, but the pursuit was delayed while they discussed who should march in front, and this gave Duchess Brownie time to cast herself before the Queen and demand a boon.

Every bride has a right to a boon, and what she asked for was Maimie's life. "Anything except that," replied Queen Mab sternly, and all the fairies echoed, "Anything except that." But when they learned how Maimie had befriended Brownie and so enabled her to attend the ball to their great glory and renown, they gave three huzzas for the little human, and set off, like an army, to thank her, the court advancing in front and the canopy keeping step with it. They traced Maimie easily by her footprints in the snow.

But though they found her deep in snow in the Figs, it seemed impossible to thank Maimie, for they could not waken her. They went through the form of thanking her—that is to say, the new King stood on her body and read her a long address of welcome, but she heard not a word of it. They also cleared the snow off her, but soon she was covered again, and they saw she was in danger of perishing of cold.

"Turn her into something that does not mind the cold," seemed a good suggestion of the doctor's, but the only thing they could think of that does not mind cold was a snowflake. "And it might melt," the Queen pointed out, so that idea had to be given up.

A magnificent attempt was made to carry her to a sheltered spot, but though there were so many of them she was too heavy. By this time all the ladies were crying in their handkerchiefs, but presently the Cupids had a lovely idea. "Build a house round her," they cried, and at once everybody perceived that this was the thing to do; in a moment a hundred fairy sawyers were among the branches, architects were running round Maimie, measuring her; a bricklayer's yard sprang up at her feet, seventy-five masons rushed up with the foundation-stone, and the Queen laid it, overseers were appointed to keep the boys off, scaffoldings were run up, the whole place rang with hammers and chisels and turning-lathes, and by this time the roof was on and the glaziers were putting in the windows.

The house was exactly the size of Maimie and perfectly lovely. One of her arms was extended, and this had bothered them for a second, but they built a verandah round it leading to the front door. The windows were the size of a coloured picture-book and the door rather smaller, but it would be easy for

Building the house for Maimie.
[See page 151.]

her to get out by taking off the roof. The fairies, as is their custom, clapped their hands with delight over their cleverness, and they were so madly in love with the little house that they could not bear to think they had finished it. So they gave it ever so many little extra touches, and even then they added more extra touches.

For instance, two of them ran up a ladder and put on a chimney.

"Now we fear it is quite finished," they sighed.

But no, for another two ran up the ladder, and tied some smoke to the chimney.

"That certainly finishes it," they cried reluctantly.

"Not at all," cried a glow-worm; "if she were to wake without seeing a night-light she might be frightened, so I shall be her night-light."

"Wait one moment," said a china merchant, "and I shall make you a saucer."

Now, alas! it was absolutely finished.

Oh, dear no!

"Gracious me!" cried a brass manufacturer, "there's no handle on the door," and he put one on.

An ironmonger added a scraper, and an old lady ran up with a door-mat. Carpenters arrived with a water-butt, and the painters insisted on painting it.

Finished at last!

"Finished! how can it be finished," the plumber demanded scornfully, "before hot and cold are put in?" and he put in hot and cold. Then an army of gardeners arrived with fairy carts and spades and seeds and bulbs and forcing-houses, and soon they had a flower-garden to the right of the verandah, and a vegetable garden to the left, and roses and clematis on the walls of the house, and in less time than five minutes all these dear things were in full bloom.

Oh, how beautiful the little house was

now! But it was at last finished true as true, and they had to leave it and return to the dance. They all kissed their hands to it as they went away, and the last to go was Brownie. She stayed a moment behind the others to drop a pleasant dream down the chimney.

All through the night the exquisite little house stood there in the Figs taking care of Maimie, and she never knew. She slept until the dream was quite finished, and woke feeling deliciously cosy just as morning was breaking from its egg, and then she almost fell asleep again, and then she called out, "Tony," for she thought she was at home in the nursery. As Tony made no answer, she sat up, whereupon her head hit the roof, and it opened like the lid of a box, and to her bewilderment she saw all around her the Kensington Gardens lying deep in snow. As she was not in the nursery she wondered whether this was really herself, so she pinched her cheeks, and then she knew it was herself, and this reminded her that she was in the middle of a great adventure. She remembered now everything that had happened to her from the closing of the gates up to her running away from the fairies, but however, she asked herself, had she got into this funny place? She stepped out by the roof, right over the garden, and then she saw the dear house in which she had passed the night. It so entranced her that she could think of nothing else.

"O you darling! O you sweet! O you love!" she cried.

Perhaps a human voice frightened the little house, or maybe it now knew that its work was done, for no sooner had Maimie spoken than it began to grow smaller; it shrank so slowly that she could scarce believe it was shrinking, yet she soon knew that it could not contain her now. It always remained as complete as ever, but it became smaller and smaller, and the garden dwindled at the same time, and the snow crept closer, lapping house and garden up. Now the house was the size of a little dog's kennel, and now of a Noah's Ark, but still you could see the smoke and the door-handle and the roses on the wall, every one complete. The glow-worm light was waning too, but it was still there. "Darling, loveliest, don't go!" Maimie cried, falling on her knees, for the little house was now the size of a reel of thread, but still quite complete. But as she stretched out her arms imploringly the snow crept up on all sides until it met itself, and where the little house had been was now one unbroken expanse of snow.

Maimie stamped her foot naughtily, and was putting her fingers to her eyes, when she heard a kind voice say, "Don't cry, pretty human, don't cry," and then she turned round and saw a beautiful little naked boy regarding her wistfully. She knew at once that he must be Peter Pan.

VI
Peter's Goat

Maimie felt quite shy, but Peter knew not what shy was.

"I hope you have had a good night," he said earnestly.

"Thank you," she replied, "I was so cosy and warm. But you"—and she looked at his nakedness awkwardly—"don't you feel the least bit cold?"

Now cold was another word Peter had forgotten, so he answered, "I think not, but I may be wrong: you see I am rather ignorant. I am not exactly a boy; Solomon says I am a Betwixt-and-Between."

"So that is what it is called," said Maimie thoughtfully.

"That's not my name," he explained, "my name is Peter Pan."

"Yes, of course," she said, "I know, everybody knows."

You can't think how pleased Peter was to learn that all the people outside the gates knew about him. He begged Maimie to tell him what they knew and what they said, and she did so. They were sitting by this time on a fallen tree; Peter had cleared off the snow for Maimie, but he sat on a snowy bit himself.

"Squeeze closer," Maimie said.

"What is that?" he asked, and she showed him, and then he did it. They talked together and he found that people knew a great deal about him, but not everything, not that he had gone back to his mother and been barred out, for instance, and he said nothing of this to Maimie, for it still humiliated him.

"Do they know that I play games exactly like real boys?" he asked very proudly. "O Maimie, please tell them!" But when he revealed how he played, by sailing his hoop on the Round Pond, and so on, she was simply horrified.

"All your ways of playing," she said with her big eyes on him, "are quite, quite wrong, and not in the least like how boys play."

Poor Peter uttered a little moan at this, and he cried for the first time for I know not how long. Maimie was extremely sorry for him, and lent him her handkerchief, but he didn't know in the least what to do with it, so she showed him, that is to say, she wiped her eyes, and then gave it back to him, saying "Now you do it," but instead of wiping his own eyes he wiped hers, and she thought it best to pretend that this was what she had meant.

She said out of pity for him, "I shall give you a kiss if you like," but though he once knew, he had long forgotten what kisses are, and he replied, "Thank you," and held out his hand, thinking she had offered to put something into it. This was a great shock to her, but she felt she could not explain without shaming him, so with charming delicacy she gave Peter a thimble which happened to be in her pocket, and pretended that it was a kiss. Poor little boy! he quite believed her, and to this day he wears it on his finger, though there can be scarcely any one who needs a thimble so little. You see, though still a tiny child, it was really years and years since he had seen his mother, and I dare say the baby who had supplanted him was now a man with whiskers.

But you must not think that Peter Pan was a boy to pity rather than to admire; if Maimie began by thinking this, she soon found she was very much mistaken. Her eyes glistened with admiration when he told her of his adventures, especially of how he went to and fro between the island and the Gardens in the Thrush's Nest.

"How romantic!" Maimie exclaimed, but it was another unknown word, and he hung his head thinking she was despising him.

"I suppose Tony would not have done

that?" he said very humbly.

"Never, never!" she answered with conviction, "he would have been afraid."

"What is afraid?" asked Peter longingly. He thought it must be some splendid thing. "I do wish you would teach me how to be afraid, Maimie," he said.

"I believe no one could teach that to you," she answered adoringly, but Peter thought she meant that he was stupid. She had told him about Tony and of the wicked thing she did in the dark to frighten him (she knew quite well that it was wicked), but Peter misunderstood her meaning and said, "Oh, how I wish I was as brave as Tony!"

It quite irritated her. "You are twenty thousand times braver than Tony," she said; "you are ever so much the bravest boy I ever knew."

He could scarcely believe she meant it, but when he did believe he screamed with joy.

"And if you want very much to give me a

kiss," Maimie said, "you can do it."

Very reluctantly Peter began to take the thimble off his finger. He thought she wanted it back.

"I don't mean a kiss," she said hurriedly, "I mean a thimble."

"What's that?" Peter asked.

"It's like this," she said, and kissed him.

"I should love to give you a thimble," Peter said gravely, so he gave her one. He gave her quite a number of thimbles, and then a delightful idea came into his head. "Maimie," he said, "will you marry me?"

Now, strange to tell, the same idea had come at exactly the same time into Maimie's head. "I should like to," she answered, "but will there be room in your boat for two?"

"If you squeeze close," he said eagerly.

"Perhaps the birds would be angry?"

He assured her that the birds would love to have her, though I am not so certain of it myself. Also that there were very few birds in winter. "Of course they might want your clothes," he had to admit rather falteringly.

She was somewhat indignant at this.

"They are always thinking of their nests," he said apologetically, "and there are some bits of you"—he stroked the fur on her pelisse—"that would excite them very much."

"They shan't have my fur," she said sharply.

"No," he said, still fondling it, however, "no. O Maimie," he said rapturously, "do you know why I love you? It is because you are like a beautiful nest."

Somehow this made her uneasy. "I think you are speaking more like a bird than a boy now," she said, holding back, and indeed he was even looking rather like a bird. "After all," she said, "you are only a Betwixt-and-Between." But it hurt him so much that she immediately added, "It must be a delicious thing to be."

"Come and be one, then, dear Maimie,"

he implored her, and they set off for the boat, for it was now very near Open-Gate time. "And you are not a bit like a nest," he whispered to please her.

"But I think it is rather nice to be like one," she said in a woman's contradictory way. "And, Peter, dear, though I can't give them my fur, I wouldn't mind their building in it. Fancy a nest in my neck with little spotty eggs in it! O Peter, how perfectly lovely!"

But as they drew near the Serpentine, she shivered a little, and said, "Of course I shall go and see mother often, quite often. It is not as if I was saying good-bye for ever to mother, it is not in the least like that."

"Oh no," answered Peter, but in his heart he knew it was very like that, and he would have told her so had he not been in a quaking fear of losing her. He was so fond of her, he felt he could not live without her. "She will forget her mother in time, and be happy with me," he kept saying to himself, and he hurried her on, giving her thimbles by the way.

But even when she had seen the boat and exclaimed ecstatically over its loveliness, she still talked tremblingly about her mother. "You know quite well, Peter, don't you," she said, "that I wouldn't come unless I knew for certain I could go back to mother whenever I want to? Peter, say it."

He said it, but he could no longer look her in the face.

"If you are sure your mother will always want you," he added rather sourly.

"The idea of mother's not always wanting me!" Maimie cried, and her face glistened.

"If she doesn't bar you out," said Peter huskily.

"The door," replied Maimie, "will always, always be open, and mother will always be waiting at it for me."

"Then," said Peter, not without grimness, "step in, if you feel so sure of her," and he helped Maimie into the Thrush's Nest.

"But why don't you look at me?" she asked, taking him by the arm.

Peter tried hard not to look, he tried to push off, then he gave a great gulp and jumped ashore and sat down miserably in the snow.

She went to him. "What is it, dear, dear Peter?" she said, wondering.

"O Maimie," he cried, "it isn't fair to take you with me if you think you can go back! Your mother"—he gulped again—"you don't know them as well as I do."

And then he told her the woeful story of how he had been barred out, and she gasped all the time. "But my mother," she said, "*my* mother——"

"Yes, she would," said Peter, "they are all the same. I dare say she is looking for another one already."

Maimie said aghast, "I can't believe it. You see, when you went away your mother had none, but my mother has Tony, and surely they are satisfied when they have one."

Peter replied bitterly, "You should see the letters Solomon gets from ladies who have six."

Just then they heard a grating *creak,* followed by *creak, creak,* all round the Gardens. It was the Opening of the Gates, and Peter jumped nervously into his boat. He knew Maimie would not come with him now, and he was trying bravely not to cry. But Maimie was sobbing painfully.

"If I should be too late," she said in agony, "O Peter, if she has got another one already!"

Again he sprang ashore as if she had called him back. "I shall come and look for you to-night," he said, squeezing close, "but if you hurry away I think you will be in time."

Then he pressed a last thimble on her sweet little mouth, and covered his face with his hands so that he might not see her go.

"Dear Peter!" she cried.

"Dear Maimie!" cried the tragic boy.

She leapt into his arms, so that it was a sort of fairy wedding, and then she hurried away. Oh, how she hastened to the gates! Peter, you may be sure, was back in the Gardens that night as soon as Lock-out sounded, but he found no Maimie, and so he knew she had been in time. For long he hoped that some night she would come back to him; often he thought he saw her waiting for him by the shore of the Serpentine as his bark drew to land, but Maimie never went back. She wanted to, but she was afraid that if she saw her dear Betwixt-and-Between again she would linger with him too long, and besides the ayah now kept a sharp eye on her. But she often talked lovingly of Peter, and she knitted a kettle-holder for him, and one day when she was wondering what Easter present he would like, her mother made a suggestion.

"Nothing," she said thoughtfully, "would be so useful to him as a goat."

"He could ride on it," cried Maimie, "and play on his pipe at the same time."

"Then," her mother asked, "won't you give him your goat, the one you frighten Tony with at night?"

"But it isn't a real goat," Maimie said.

"It seems very real to Tony," replied her mother.

"It seems frightfully real to me too," Maimie admitted, "but how could I give it to Peter?"

Her mother knew a way, and next day, accompanied by Tony (who was really quite a nice boy, though of course he could not compare), they went to the Gardens, and Maimie stood alone within a fairy ring, and then her mother, who was a rather gifted lady, said—

"My daughter, tell me, if you can,
What have you got for Peter Pan?"

To which Maimie replied—

"I have a goat for him to ride,
Observe me cast it far and wide."

She then flung her arms about as if she were sowing seed, and turned round three times.

Next Tony said—

"If P. doth find it waiting here,
Wilt ne'er again make me to fear?"

And Maimie answered—

"By dark or light I fondly swear
Never to see goats anywhere."

She also left a letter to Peter in a likely place, explaining what she had done, and begging him to ask the fairies to turn the goat into one convenient for riding on. Well, it all happened just as she hoped, for Peter found the letter, and of course nothing could be easier for the fairies than to turn the goat into a real one, and so that is how Peter got the goat on which he now rides round the Gardens every night playing sublimely on his pipe. And Maimie kept her promise, and never frightened Tony with a goat again, though I have heard that she created another animal. Until she was quite a big girl she continued to leave presents for Peter in the Gardens (with letters explaining how humans play with them), and she is not the only one who has done this. David does it, for instance, and he and I know the likeliest place for leaving them in, and we shall tell you if you like, but for mercy's sake don't ask us before Porthos, for he is so fond of toys that, were he to find out the place, he would take every one of them.

Though Peter still remembers Maimie he is become as gay as ever, and often in sheer happiness he jumps off his goat and lies kicking merrily on the grass. Oh, he has a joyful time! But he has still a vague memory that he was a human once, and it makes him especially kind to the house-swallows when they visit the island, for house-swallows are the spirits of little children who have died. They always build in the eaves of the houses where they lived when they were humans, and sometimes they try to fly in at a nursery window, and perhaps that is why Peter loves them best of all the birds.

And the little house? Every lawful night (that is to say, every night except ball nights) the fairies now build the little house lest there should be a human child lost in the Gardens, and Peter rides the marshes looking for lost ones, and if he finds them he carries them on his goat to the little house, and when they wake up they are in it, and when they step out they see it. The fairies build the house merely because it is so pretty, but Peter rides round in memory of Maimie, and because he still loves to do just as he believes real boys would do.

But you must not think that, because somewhere among the trees the little house is twinkling, it is a safe thing to remain in the Gardens after Lock-out time. If the bad ones among the fairies happen to be out that night they will certainly mischief you, and even though they are not, you may perish of cold and dark before Peter Pan comes round. He has been too late several times, and when he

If the bad ones among the fairies happen to be out.
[See page 173.]

They will certainly mischief you.
[See page 173.]

sees he is too late he runs back to the Thrush's Nest for his paddle, of which Maimie had told him the true use, and he digs a grave for the child and erects a little tombstone, and carves the poor thing's initials on it. He does this at once because he thinks it is what real boys would do, and you must have noticed the little stones, and that there are always two together. He puts them in twos because it seems less lonely. I think that quite the most touching sight in the Gardens is the two tombstones of Walter Stephen Matthews and Phoebe Phelps. They stand together at the spot where the parish of Westminster St. Mary's is said to meet the Parish of Paddington. Here Peter found the two babes, who had fallen unnoticed from their perambulators, Phoebe aged thirteen months and Walter probably still younger, for Peter seems to have felt a delicacy about putting any age on his stone. They lie side by side, and the simple inscriptions read

<table><tr><td>W.

St. M.</td><td>and</td><td>13a
P. P.
1841.</td></tr></table>

David sometimes places white flowers on these two innocent graves.

But how strange for parents, when they hurry into the Gardens at the opening of the gates looking for their lost one, to find the sweetest little tombstone instead. I do hope that Peter is not too ready with his spade. It is all rather sad.

I think that quite the most touching sight in the Gardens is the two tombstones of Walter Stephen Matthews and Phoebe Phelps.
[See page 176.]